minedition

North American edition published 2019 by Michael Neugebauer Publishing Ltd. Hong Kong

Text copyright © 2010 by Géraldine Elschner
Illustrations copyright © 2010 by Eve Tharlet
English text adaption by Kathryn Bishop
Rights arranged with "minedition" Rights and Licensing AG, Zurich, Switzerland.

Michael Neugebauer Publishing Ltd.,
Unit 28, 5/F, Metro Centre, Phase 2, No.21 Lam Hing Street, Kowloon Bay, Kowloon, Hong Kong
Phone: +852 2807 1711, e-mail: info@minedition.com
This book was printed in August 2018 at L.Rex Ltd
3/F., Blue Box Factory Building, 25 Hing Wo Street, Tin Wan, Aberdeen, Hong Kong, China
Typesetting in Kidprint.
Library of Congress Cataloging-in-Publication Data available upon request.

ISBN 978-988-8341-74-0
10 9 8 7 6 5 4 3 2 1
First Impression

For more information please visit our website: www.minedition.com

MY Little Chick

From Egg to Chick...

Géraldine Elschner
illustrated by Eve Tharlet
translated by Kathryn Bishop

minedition

"Cock-a-doodle-doo!" crows the rooster happily as I arrive at the farmyard this morning. If I imagine hard enough he almost seems to call my name—Lena. The hens cluck around him, marching back and forth. Suzy scratches about in the dust, and Alma pecks at a seed here and a piece of grass there.

But something feels like it's missing... Where are all the fluffy little chicks, so soft and warm? I hope one comes soon.

But Mom tells me, "To get a chick the hen has to mate with the rooster. After she's laid her egg she has to sit on it for 21 days."

I want to find out when the next chick will hatch, so I lift the latch and slip into the henhouse.

Inside it's warm and muggy. A strong musty smell fills the room and a pale light shines through the little window in the roof. I creep behind the bales of hay and wait, quiet as a mouse.

Finally, the little door-flap opens and there's Alma, looking soft and as white as a pillow. With a flap of her wings she flies down to land on her nest. I hold my breath.

For what seems a very long time Alma just sits in the straw, as still as a statue.

Then she fluffs herself up, squeezes, and presses—and there, underneath her back feathers, appears a small white thing.

My eyes open wide.

The white thing grows bigger and bigger, and suddenly...

PLOP!

An egg lands in the straw.
How wonderful...!
I can hardly believe my eyes.
Now Alma just has to sit on her egg.

But what's this?

Instead of sitting on
her egg, Alma gives
a loud "cluck, cluck"
and proudly leaves
the henhouse.

What now?

Quickly I scamper over
and pick up the egg.
It's warm, slightly damp
and shiny.

"You'll get cold in there all alone,"
I whisper to the chick.
"I'll have to help hatch you."

Holding the egg carefully,
I go back into the house
and climb into bed.

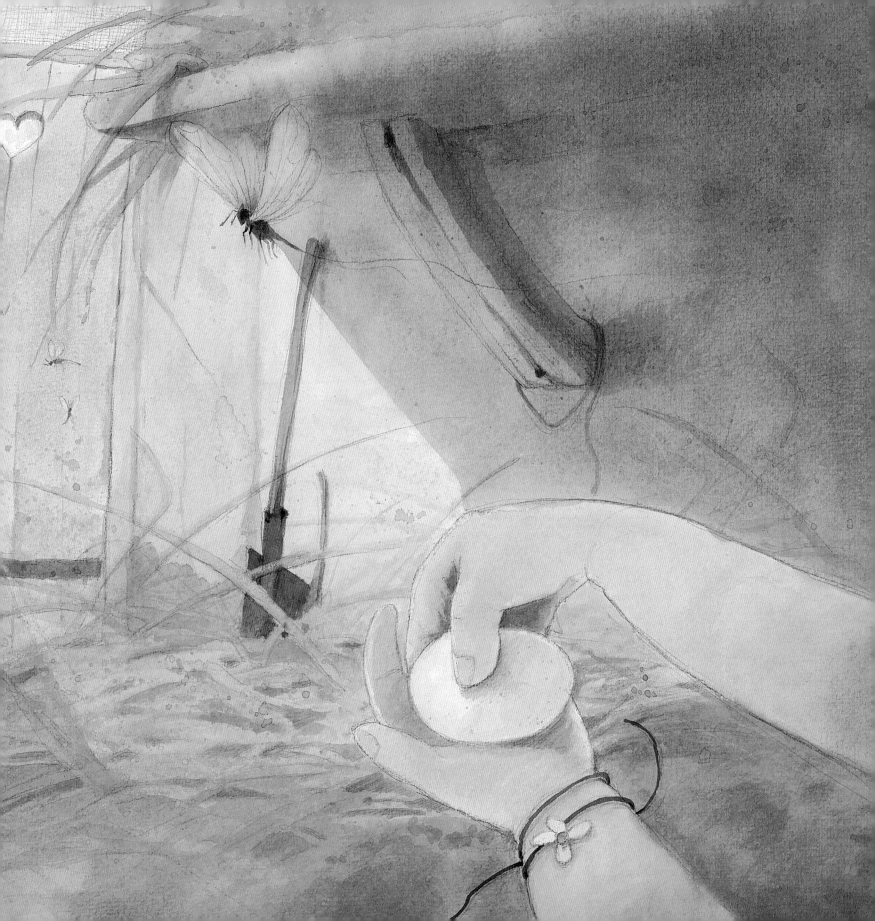

One blanket, two blankets-more!
I need lots of blankets if the little chick
is to stay warm in here for 21 days.

I'll have to be very patient.
Then I'll be able to surprise
everyone with my own little chick!

My mom sees me and looks worried.
"Lena, are you ill? Maybe I should take
your temperature." So I decide to get
out of bed and sneak my egg toward
the living room couch, when suddenly
I bump into my dad...

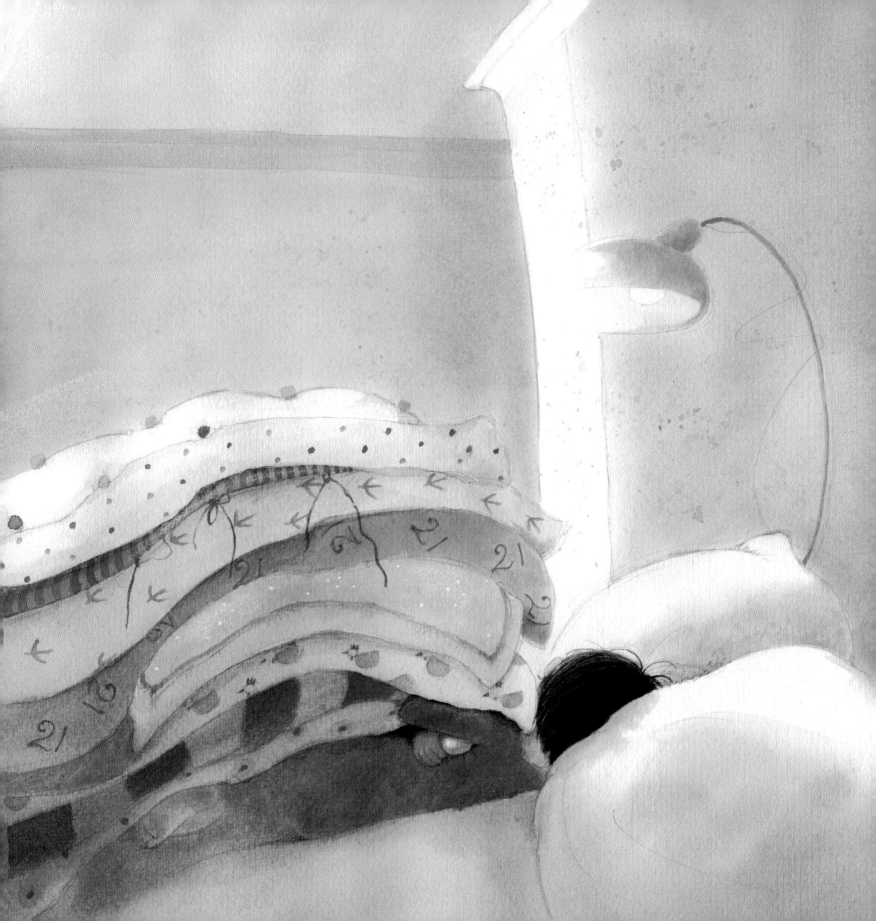

...who lifts me up and swings me around.
It's my favorite game, but not today...

S P L A T !

We all look at the floor in surprise.
"My little chick!"
I cry, barely able to see it
through my tears.

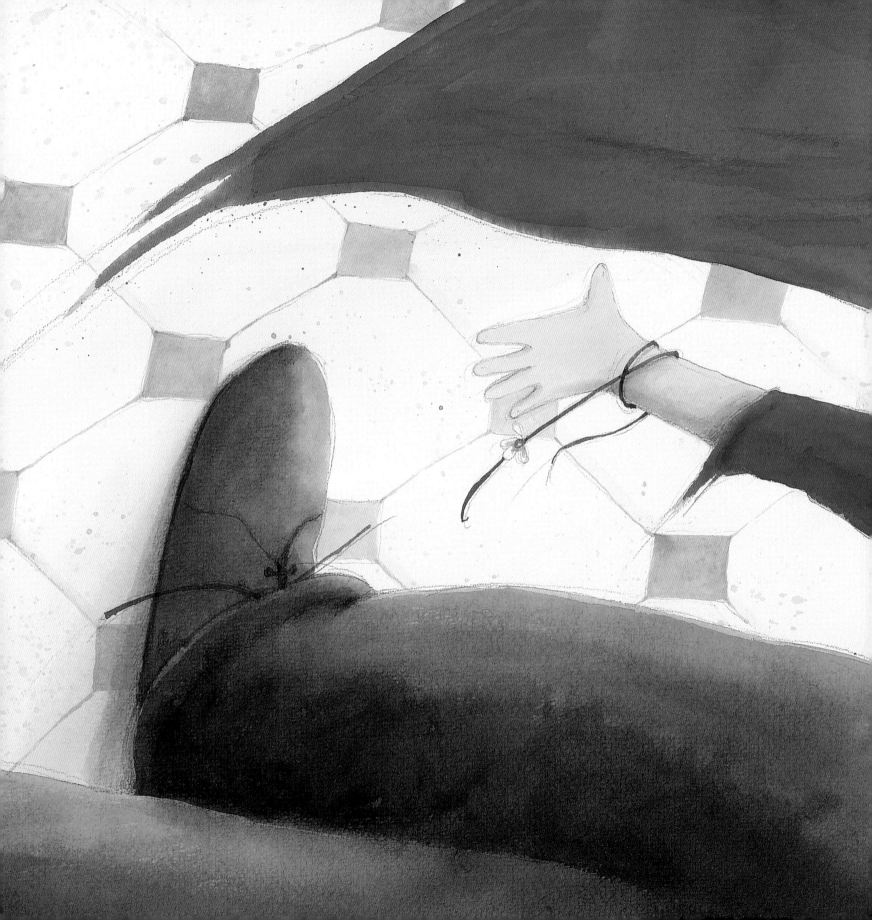

"It wasn't a chick, not yet anyway,"
my mom explains after I tell her what happened earlier.
"It's not that easy to hatch an egg. Sometimes they don't hatch
at all. Hens are best at it; otherwise you need an incubator."
"An incubator?"

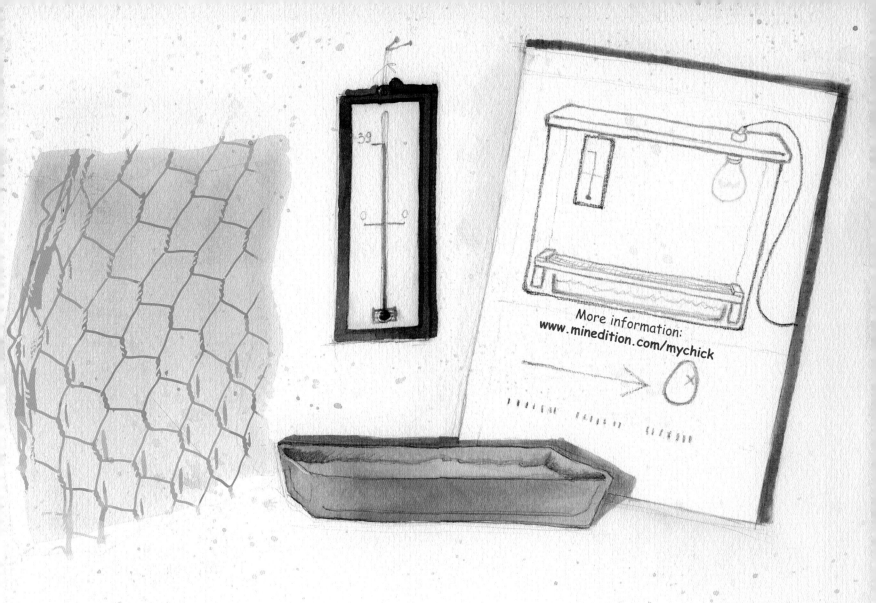

More information:
www.minedition.com/mychick

"That's a small box where it stays warm," my brother Theo says.
"They're not hard to build. Let's make one!"

My tears dry up and we all set to work. Mom finds the instructions,
and Dad and Theo get the materials. Two days later the special box
is ready. All we need is an egg. Will Alma lay another one soon?

At last! Will the egg be warm enough,

as warm as under Alma's feathers?

Every morning
I carefully turn the egg.

┼┼┼┼ ‖

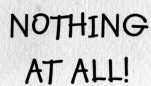

And turn...

┼┼┼┼ ‖‖‖

┼┼┼┼ ┼┼┼┼ ‖‖‖

NOTHING
AT ALL!

┼┼┼┼ ┼┼┼┼ ‖‖‖‖

Is anything living in that egg?
I wish I could see inside.

┼┼┼┼ ┼┼┼┼ ┼┼┼┼

┼┼┼┼ ┼┼┼┼ ┼┼┼┼ ‖‖‖

I may have to give up.
Then I spot a tiny crack...

┼┼┼┼ ┼┼┼┼ ┼┼┼┼ ┼┼┼┼

┼┼┼┼ ┼┼┼┼ ┼┼┼┼ ┼┼┼┼‖

Finally, the cute little chick
is in my hand, so soft, so
sweet—what a wonder!
I stroke its golden down for
a long time.

Then I bring it back to Alma.
My little chick may be happy
with me, but it'll be happiest
of all under its mother's warm
feathers... and with the rest
of its brothers and sisters!